THE
LITTLE
COMPANION

CAROLINE MACLEOD

Printed in the United States of America
Library of Congress Control Number: 2024920290
ISBN: Softcover   979-8-89518-312-0
            e-Book   979-8-89518-313-7
Published by: WP Lighthouse
Publication Date: 09/24/2024

To buy a copy of this book, please contact:
WP Lighthouse
Phone: +1-888-668-2459
support@wplighthouse.com
wplighthouse.com

CONTENTS

Murder One 1

Listing 3

No Title 4

Love 5

Catch the Cat 6

Antennas 7

The Revelation...8

The Morning...9

Family 10

Teaching the Mask 11

Ferry NorthStar 12

Stag and Bore 14

Ganglanders 31

Republican Rites 32

Mental 34

The Certain Time 35

Men... 36

Perception 37

Major Tom 38

Coming Home 39

Fellowship 40

Media Failure 41

See to Blink 42

Hungary Budapest 43

The path of Life 44

Fires 45

Delivered... 46

All Happy 48

Travelling Communion.. 49

Expression 50

Home 51

Difference.. 54

Lucy Letby 55

Saying no to sex is hard and the body is defiant in its advances to get the hormones back again especially experienced as a board as I am myself.

Wooden doorstep and watering hole also the butt.

We are all also at longered and Angeles for some.

Sex is a funny aspect to love in that it is exceptional for questions and order in the contact details of my lessons absent from stage school.

Saying no to that honey feeling is the worst and loss-some to my brain as shock of denial therefore vanity to pretty in ugliness of self-catering looks to thin the ice on which I struggle in the definate water.

Sleeping well.

Murder One

· · · · · · · · · · ·

Murder One is a dark will that can be chucked out at your own discretion. Some men may not be willing to do this because of their disturbed layering. Preening of those layers is the first step towards calming down; and reasserting your own control to kick out the dark will. Some men like to live within this dark will because they have negative behavioural problems, associated with fear of solitude from associated bullying. This is very gregarious and causes the hate of contact for some men and women in speech. They will have already crabbed-in their fear of social aggressiveness. It is a call to alms for the middle east. People love being helped and this is why we get the best World by helping people disassociate from their happiness and regain neutral control. In this unbattered state they regain some of their insight and stay safe in their penetrative disassociated thoughts of their disturbed normal behaviour thus remaining benign and safe to everyone as non-existent.

This is normal for them to reach in understanding who in the World is around them.

Murder two is when people have a pan-quicked fear of courage and loss of total realities. Thereable, to flee is not an issue, describes the mind of them. This describes the thought process of flight being denied access to them and their courage is to follow them to deal with the ensued form of their mind, to engage them in a different way, so being trained, in this way, they will still not alleviate murder if they become muddled.

Murder, two, too, is the same lack of flight but the fear of solitude to them so they will murder to keep a safe place in their heart for a person.

Don't lose your order. Formation of order is the basis of army training. Order one.

Murder three is about death or loss of limb, each being the same thing, occurring by accidental deterrents.

Here I am explaining degrees.

LISTING
· · · · · ·

There are days where the low cloud feels my moody language.

Listing years upon year of up and down moods, following unexplained skip to the games my fair maiden highs of extremity.

The lure of lying flat on my bed grips me when the clock strikes 3.03pm.

Limbs aching in the endless stretch and pull.

The sanctity of 20 minutes in the brief quiet of relax.

Drifting back in to the living room where my husband is resting and feeling fear of solitude instead of listening to the television.

Filling my day with call-outs of sentences and sound, I lift my cup of tea, and to my surprise I find this blend comforting, kindish, rising and belonging.

No Title
· · · · · · ·

Today is a good day. I am cared for and look to a better sunset. Childhood was an army exercise as my parents decided their course was to be special in my development.

Here I share within my abilities of media the personality straits of the world.

The comedy of life I bring to you.

Nice people are the fog and aim the darkness, the non seeing light in their World as if others are the cause, as sensitive people, to take their emotional war.

The point and prod of rules and lack of expectancy are ours because we do not see anything but light work or prayer. This is true.

Degree Learning

Murder One is a dark will that can be chucked out at your own discretion. Some men may not be willing to do this because of their disturbed layering. Preening of those layers is the first step towards calming down; and reasserting your own control to kick out the dark will. Some men like to live within this dark will because they have negative behavioural problems, associated with fear of solitude from associated bullying. This is very gregarious and causes the hate of contact for some men and women in speech. People love being helped and this is why we get the best World by helping people.

LOVE

• • •

Because you have met in your innocence a relationship is in death.

Love behold thy conquerer of eros statue march.

We cannot wait until death has past.

Truth is we live in the love of living and love each other living.

We don't know how long our love will last.

But in marriage there is a commitment to live unto death to us has past.

You do not start again when you are hit because everything shatters when you are hit by a man you love and falls to infinite dust and even the dust disappears and you don't know where it has gone.

You carry on from the hit just exactly where you are and your man will remember the sadness he has caused and in my case will not hit you ever again.

You remember your part in the cause of the hit, women, and you speak it out to him so he understands where it came from in him and he will know how to block his fight with you.

Men get carried away in their penetrative thoughts. Women play music freely to Women only.

The joy of sex, it certainly is not what love is for.

The certain bubble of softness, in a cloudy feeling, of content spheres resolving is love.

Catch the Cat

· · · · · · · · · · · · ·

I have realised the beginning of the war again as told at first and what we have been treated with via war is not what any of the religiously treated children would have wanted.

This is the circle.

Blood payment.

Ethical.

Not Moral.

Not lawful.

IT'S CHINA. A TROJAN WHO BELIEVES IN WAR FOREVERMORE.

Antennas

· · · · · · · ·

Transformer's.

Britain, Haite and Saudi Arabia.

The power source is an ADCD sockets.

My brother made me find this out as we were kids and I don't know what it knocked out when I plugged it into the socket in the house.

Saudi Arabia irrigation was shocking in the 1980's. I remember the terror of seeing the machinery closeup.

It was turned into cable fencing the like of which has caused an inconvenience in Texas Taxes. Israel are wanting the fencing but Palestinian areas want it and have a water source ISRAEL want.

Simple deal should be simple.

THE REVELATION

· · · · · · · · · · · · ·

Always Amen.

The courage to change what you can and the wisdom to know when you accept it as is.

To give up alcohol for the book of Twelve.

To realise memory is for this life only.

To remember we are all Travellers and meet eternal lives we have known in love from time to time.

To remember it is not good to have the whole world the same.

To know we live on the plates of the underlying rocks of the world all differing in the chemical makeup. People represent this in a country too country diffidence.

The Morning
· · · · · · · · · · ·

The morning was o'clock in the morning. Thay had waited until the hour for the broadcast.

She was moved to Contin.

The balance was never enough.

I experience the same thing so I can agree with her on that one then.

I follow my orders.

Chapter 1 was an order. Lecturn 21.

CAN Followed carefully the Lecturn of the college. Burswood, they called her.

She got pregnant to be closer to the Mary.

FAMILY

· · · · ·

Mood, anxiety and psychosis disorders.

Mental health has affected 3 of the people I know, including myself, George and Jenna.

George and I have been hoodwinked by Jenna who had one over on her Mother Christine and by association Paul her stepfather.

We have been treated by lenses, coloured and sight adjustment editors.

Jane, George's sister has caused a fractionalising in the family.

I don't care sometimes about nudity. Neither does George sometimes.

There is a reason that we are there therefore we are her three nuisances.

There's always a level limit. Beyond this we are mortified by Anne from Cathal.

Sigmund Ffoids was guilty and Cathal had to sign him off.

A geisha's game is being played by The Record Editor Andrews Andrew's.

Someone very lightweight in their character is falling and losing their friends.

John Bell, 250 Princes St, Edinburgh. Only cares about his own Life. He was on the same compound, pilots paradise, in Riyadh, Saudi Arabia as an intern. His wife was called Racquella and she has since died.

Life is the Amazon with our numbers as tributaries on a bed fed by foundations of which we follow one separately along with our number at birth.

TEACHING THE MASK

Teaching in the church asks us to accept all and as you reach middle life this is easy to accept when having a rough tough manners with little intervention.

Love of one kind or another or a subject instead of a person comes from within and only a mask can be taught to cover it with convention.

Accept of people of anykind is what the bible tells us to let us know convention and meets with the knowledge so far learned at years of 56.

Any love is true.

Evil is true and this is where we seek our redemption ado domini. We descent to our cleansing so far as it is individuality concerned and then rise to our fulfilment to accept our good again and from thence forth to our new beginning of light prism attraction to oxygen.

We are happy when we recognise thee god inside us. There we relax to challenge with little chides to encourage our development in whichever way we ageaon/anon.

Ferry NorthStar

• • • • • • • • • • • • • •

This could be a part of the check of the Slovenia War.

The passing of Her Majesty The Queen left us in distress at the lack of retirement now on following the pressure again as King Charles III and Princess Kate are treated for Cancer.

The jet stream is moving South East to the Eastern Block if anyone has any sense. This causes emotive responsibilities for all of us.

Storm calls after storm and the middle day of high heat is that to expect from the midnight skies.

Soft and palpable love has taken many years to come by repetition of standing here by the side of my man in marriage and mortar of our long-standing home.

The recollection of moving on tirelessly is being to cease and descending into stability of tepid stages in stagnation of recourse.

Calm dissipates the spell unearthing the man within to another motives movement.

The capability name is not within reason for know; it is there to prevent relocation reliance.

G7 and T4 in the GULF considering The West Bank Palestine and Yemen; this is intention-watched by Saudi Arabia and the GULF area and leads straight to Kuwait 8. France F9; there is a massive Arabic populus. S8 being Switzerland Silver.

Russia is the Authority at Sea this far North with the Northstar Ferry on the west coast to Ireland Stenatherne.

Charlie London cannot afford the extra Bromine the Guar from Malaysia : Therefore we are still right on track, with an attack from Russia, whom have deployed 79 missiles to Ukraine overnight. 3.A.1. Save Our Soules'; Ever present and necessary evil suffering. Suggesting it is coming from somewhere else; pertaining to the Torahs' conversation. Perhaps South America workers of The Panama Canal, together with Escher Egypt. It will be philosophical that Putin is. We need to do a deal now.

Stag and Bore
· · · · · · · · · · · ·

Since 2021 December when I thought oh, almighty goodness here we go again in our usual pattern of war and peace, it being the bloodshed of men to screw more money for the World as they are gifted to the Earth for their outer layer of being our protector.

The emotions of nerves struck last night as I shook for 25 minutes at the words of a Palestinian man saying Zepharyus in his pain and anguish at seeing rubble everywhere around him and no food for his son and no idea when and where it would be coming from. His nerves were obviously so badly shattered by then, in this persistence of battling on with no money that holding his son by the face he cursed us all with the Devil's half-brother.

We are used to seeing camps and tents with boiling pots as many people live this way anyway but not the mental instability of normal men prepared to die for us, as I have used the word myself and so have Zepharyus in me also.

My father told me he had put a plot of 4 in the surroundings for me, consider what I have lost he said to me. Many people were going to lose personalities and characters too: Consider how you behave.

Being mental health considered as too much myself to join in properly for whatever reason; this is the approach I give to myself: take your medication.

We really should take more care of ourselves Dad said. Really for us we are a very poor example.

Now, sitting here I feel, delighted and ashamed in my personal grief of having everything how I want the level to be.

My paintings journey is everything I wanted it to be. My writing is even and I am given little rewards every now and again which feed my happiness a little bit more.

I am plump which is how I like to be. I am 56 which is gaining in years a little bit. I am a little health worried which is also a sympathetic response in me. I am allowed to act out my nudity as much as I pleasure to me.

Now there is this sneaking feeling of grief as things become more intolerable to me in this War in 4 Countries over money.

The World is in loss again. I am following this loss and gaining more conscience as the days pass into months and the months into years.

A publisher rang today and asked me what I was going to write next. There has been a loose thought in my head for some time I answered; to write about the War and ask why we swap our men's blood for new money and why we in the advanced culture cannot change this pain and loss to exchange something else for the World Bank to provide extra new money allowance for us all to live on and die more naturally.

I an only me know we can do it by je sais; this comes from SACRE and this meaning LACE leads me to believe it can be achieved. People won't go blind these days. Perhaps it has a different meaning and I will endeavour to find this out. Perhaps I will try and make lace. I have learned you have to give lace; this: means freely.

Are we good enough to give Lace. PROBABLY. If so something else has gone wrong.

As I have said.

Ahh the predomination of the sentence.

We all hear this so many times when growing up. So and so's going to jail. Better believe it or otherwise you'll be going there yourself too keep them complete in their madness.

Take that as you please because my jail has been mental health.

We all have jail, inwardly. Gro-wing.

Some people live to mither and some people like to fly on a wing.

Fishing and Maw.

People want to much these days in their wait of it. The time of God to come to them.

Including Food.

This is our problem. With Britain and Israel running out of food money. This is low on our bucket list as has been said by our Government.

We are probably late on paying for our food and somewhere there is a glitch on our meat deal. Palestine are late with our mould's.

If we give up on our last meat deal we will know food poverty again.

How fair is it. Life is unfair. Not the most brilliant argument.

They seem to think Britain are better on rations for making money.

Israel are going to get our food and go to jail.

Possibly why we have been told Russia are doing a nuclear missile from Finland to Britain and Israel are; gifted a nuclear bomb.

How do we change this human consciousness to paying our food bills because otherwise we won't get food socially and this leads only to social decline.

It has been proven that people won't be separated from their money even with electricity.

I remember working life as the predomination for slight depravity creeping through me in referral to social security. This really is unpleasant as a social jurisdiction for people whom have had their choices taken from them.

It dawned on me like a star-crusading charity that cap I had to wear as ordered by the office.

There is cheats but they are naturally this way as are liars and they just find it more acceptable to tell actively.

Intuition is daunting sometimes as in lamentations. We all have these and deal with these by committing whichever solitudes occur to us. We shallow dive with food and drink to control either excessively or aggressively.

This War is all for saving money in deprivation for cheap rebuild of metal Fabrics. Perverse action was evident in the pictures of an embattled Ukraine in grey just as we see now in the West of Gaza.

We know theirs will be spiralling jets over the North Atlantic. We wonder if we will be neutral because Switzerland is having financial insurance difficulties.

Does this not fight with transport leading to stagnate and the disregard of Polish Drivers to return to our Country of Britain to work where accelerated payments go through on automation. Traffic cameras everywhere have been a good condition for referring money.

Taiwan Emilia: The importance of adding to our amount of interest off by paying more in order to survive in monetary policy. Pinhole cameras describe this very well as withholding.

I wonder at my thoughts of nuclear exhibitionism so easily deployed at the will so determined by je sais, lace, SACRE. A Lady so determined by invigorating two dead particles; their stuccato of atmospheric pressure relieved by only a simple strong silver with nitrogen.

It perhaps is not so unreasonable to have kept our countryside free from nitrates in fertiliser.

The dispute of Trade brique the which of worth we are not pear the couples in love with the social complex, a theory experiment in housing by le corbusier.

The layers of repetition to make a soft and palpable enduring in-love. I am wondering at the loss of that the panic of broken houses settles-in.

Where is the recollection and the point of departure in the sphere of the love to rebirth in this lightest of molecules; the joy and the merriment.

See this phenomena again in your evilities and cross either side of the path because neither way is wrong. The end points the yolk of yoke in this tyrant of love.

When I think of the Eastern battle of broken homes and there lifetime loss I am wondering of the panic that in-settles to make a life of new confines from nothingness.

I have taken the time over the last two years to come to terms with my evilities and this recognition helps me to move on within, regardless if I confuse myself the grapple is to reach out for that loss of personal confusion and see the credit of myself, without having to answer to the society normal.

As the dusts remain high there is a repetitive syndrome step of assault on breathing muscles which considers death in the West as a target soluble for the World; An aspirin to death. This is a normal being of time and place and indication. Where there is desert you watch the sands. Farewell to Mecca and the Reuse beyond, there was shadow in the burning earth.

The golden fingers where we use to much silver and so metal to the Earth goes on until one day there is another formulating of bolster to stop us taking directly from the ground floor of our house. Plate Tectonic disturbances will not be displayed forecast as to do or die. We can learn that it takes two weeks to settlement and leave the floors alone.

Russia are refinance in modern culture for use of all to continue in solitude and heartbroken more, money being making revenue to do it twice because the United Kingdom own part of the U.S.S.R.

We have contained guilty that thee be and themselves yourselves to a level review of ourselves and we will go to accept our evilities as natural in each of us.

This World works on Hate, Like, Black and Light and is called HAITE/

LOVE. This is our get out clause and is represented by the number 9 in Recollective Reveries or Lamentations.

Choose a job you wish for and take the financial responsibilities of surefire loss because some people want discontent and will find the way to impose their lives conditions in their outer world in which you are contained; Power-sharing is their wishlist.

We are although some people are aloof and see themselves above this; all rats in the kingdom of the Devil trained to our own choices being intelligent creatures and being given our own number to live to including those of crook or crim where their thee physically stands.

In women thee power is in their stomach which is where they say to win your man you feed their stomach: With thee.

The feeling of loss in a man is correctly expressed as lost being grumpy and sweetness lost. The words here are UT CUTIE DESTONY. This is overcome to the evenly level plateaux by falling the diaphragm in and huttering.

Flower pot man is so simple that the reverberations in time cause us to implode like the explosion ignition point of our incantation into human life of nuclear fusion in three times mieosis. In the brain in adult life this causes stagnant life. Our society equation is within us and is being levelled up so they can legally kill us all as themselves and in any depiction they wish to use on us.

Disoillusion will happen when we each of us in our individuality decide to commit suicide as in ISRAEL at the moment 2024 with the West Gaza and now entering the Lebanon; and as in RUSSIA and the Ukraine and an individual reaches this point of place in time when the reverberations reach the destruction of self centre.

Yourself in men is in the protective outer layer of thinking him as ss man. The third circle is love in evolution to omit suicide. Enterturing the second and third circle whatever you see it is as it, is the first circle of evalution; the second being timing. This will determine you to stay alive instead of being suicide you will find an answer to accept instead and in time you will forget and forgive by Mon droite meaning by your rite 4 Barlycorn smigs CHESS CQQ is how to get over mortal killing in military; actions rye's and live.

January 2023

Germany are deploying tanks to The Ukraine and its said they are not all fighting the same way which is why negotiations are like in the noonday Sun. So they will be requiring smigs to.

Religious LEE Feelings concur sex with a called spit. This includes the Religious woman SAUL in thee reference. She wanted to much for her son so she could be an equal power to him however in this cold spirit she could not still her emotional sense of power and his power of protection of his own body first and thus revealed he the greater power he had that she could not equal, therefore on the cross was he to accompany Jesus and Paul as SAUL in name only. Lamentations are for all of us as she wept at the foot of the three of them, all contained in one spirit.

The Church is there to give you the light back into your prism which dark swirls of oxygen have taken from you as this oxygenated prism is the foundation of all your life-force.

This is honey; the effect of healing the mind, the brain and body. This is recompense only. We live in stagnate evalution as simple people in which we have a crewed from globe implosion therefore acquiring the word a to describe a noun which we own however we do not own our freehold.

Stone Age equals a time of reiteration. We have had to run into depression via LIZZ TRUSS and KWASI KWARTENG which was a brave move from The Late Queen. Needing to repair is a gift truly wonderful and it works backwards, backwards reverses. Reveries of time spent. The Brexit and Covid-19 costs are a Pillion with Interests on top and we have to pay in seccies refunds at the lowest levels. Their Trichot is their problem regarding Russia: Thricot Portmanteau Trichot.

It started with the toll bar toll zerooed and Passes Next being zeroed.

Logistics is why the Jewish Meat is Levieed Free and it should be x3. The ethics reason is loss at gaming. Money to feed an apnoea comes at a cost of using the wrong word when doing things for a living as in the Post Office scandal. Unless you learn to speak at your own loss there is a good chance you won't be able to organise your own daily calendar. Vanity in depression is usually spent in losing everything to addiction of one form or another as happened to the Pure Party in repentance.

This life is taught so in its uncaught state it is unlovable to the self to learn a hard mistake. Learning however can come from a kind stranger to the family, giving you a chance call of accomplishments to control the fear to committing whichever suicide you take action to rest including your evilities, which are a learning of to control the evil raging from outside sources. We all get something to irritate our bad humour. Runaway is true of life and in many strengths of direction we all do this even in the smoking and drinking of our digestive tracts.

Our coercive communications culture has advanced us enough to not want living with open combative remarks about our own-in-fighting; References to missing children working in gangs for our farming police. They learn the language words which are separated from their punches and recalled they will not be ours again. Words are combative and little reasons prevent us from reaching to accept ourselves readily in humour because levels of useless words keep us to a high wall to negotiate with our honesty.

Please take our guilt as a moment of our appreciation of you and pay us your-own-all dividends. Bacchus needs to be paid for. Have a sip 4 times a day tells us to go lose ourselves to the love of yourselves unto death.

Ever on-living the Maw and more of ours own earth, which is incidentally tipped over us when we die as we go to soil daily. There is usually account for that but as I unknowingly it, we all go down to get cleansing before we rise again to the goodness of the stratosphere from where we descend again in the form of Christ Jesus, with another Mary mother; being a verses of Black Mary. It means a very slow, very lower standard.

The upper echelons decide our weighs and they dictate to govern us all, through our evilities. We all decry and have secrecy while we put the drink on the table as to what this question is about for honesty in us.

Yesterday there was a family in the West Bank making crisps and they were asked what their reaction would be if someone paid by giving them a bullet instead of money. A very sad inditement and the little girl said she would go away and think about it then.

We have heard the fight is about money over cable. In reality the Palestinian said no first but by invading Israel they have incurred hell haters by moving the fight onwards.

Everything is staged so it can bring the mind down to depression in which merrily we live; anger, fatigue, nowhere to reside.

Israel are not going to stop because they have on-decree; meaning payment on demand.

So the West is helping on two sides of the fight. The War is a negotiation, in the noonday Sun.

Farmers walk unto their death as do Jewish people showing their companionship in the flat they wear on their head. Perhaps they have the reason to eat dead children because of this companionship taken in a different meaning in Britain.

We have been given information that France has had a farmers riots and this is in a agroculture from where we have donned the word humanitarian as a level guiding for amount of pesticides in seedbasis. Where this is inconfusion is aid giving to the crisis of Palestine.

Our Country is on a War footing at the moment however we are not knowing which two situations in the World are going to be aiding first. We have struck the Houthis in the Yemen due to it's attacks in the sea, on supply ships to the West Bank Palestine. The Lebanon have also come under fire from us, Britain footing the bill.

So we are redeemed, all of us. This is a certainty of death culture we recognise. So for the edge of circumstance we may all be at the hangman's noose; therefore I conclude the prison for life instead of the Capital punishment. The states in the USA use evangelism to entertain the state of capit; for the use of extra money from the World Bank which incurs our World inflation rate.

The business middle men who need flamboyance has to be paid for by men and women going to their death; for them we question the need of showing more acquisitions; which we all aspire for in one way or another, so we have created our own circle of life and death so the force above us all is negotiable and it is within us all; by conception containing this power of us and to us.

We need to get on with the stage to accepting a hug and kiss between men as not gaye. It is a brother only feeling and comes from brother in us all or even son; in us all. This is not To be mixcd up with Jese Christ in anyway. In all of us in religion this is human form saturation where we reach out to negiate our losing fight within. Quieted by our fight in whichever fight it is; This is our why we live to slightly; being a quieter sense to go with our ordinary genetic depression.

Miscomprehension of gaining or losing is the fundamental win in life. Concentrating in where is leads us into our peace of us and we are in three as in the holy trinity.

Time leads us to believe confusion of things being put down to aside to deal with later. There becomes a mental hold to the brain and this together with tic tok pills makes us need a new medicating and time to digress. We at any time in our lives may go through windows epochs unsettling through beat us to the level of hospital treatments, called rest space.

We are arguing to give Israel rest space through negotiations of firing. The Ramadan period of 6 weeks is coming up soon and Palestine needs recoup. This is why Israel might be receiving the atom bomb from Russia.

Glancing back from the World War II where 30,000 Jewish people marched to their own deaths accordingly and without hesitation we come to think of the mass decision made between a conglomeration of people.

There was a shit in a puddle and it was nerves a bad one and it was aye. This is describing larger people who need wiping. They don't care about toiletry needs; even of the wheyes. Its about being at larger, to be seen as the biggest birds on the block which again goes back to historically 19th century.

Russia sent oil to Kirkwall in 2021 December and it has been therefore to come to Lovhinver for which there is a place for police presence now. This harbour makes the full diamond shape. Time is of a strange consequence when the War is finished before the negotiations began.

The deal is already underway as in the Americans making sure of the continued safety of their diplomats in West Ukraine; the deal coming from the interest repayment repayment from America to Britain. The payment being recovered in oil revenue.

Vladimir Putin was showing his strong hand in knowing the dispute would be settled anyway in what it was; it should be because it was about logistics, meaning a few people put to prison for corruption and that's all it was that made trade to expensive, for everyone.

Every now and then trade goes wrong and we have got to fix the problem. There afore gives us the lengths of custody which are to be dealt with for those men and women acaught in the logistics fiasco. Problems in this is that there will be other corded reasons for punishments.

Such as taking your husband or wife in full knowledge of what they have done as in innocence to you and that they are the best for you to stand along. We need to know what the senior clergymen mean by expediency, for when they take over the Country to bring it down to God. We will not know to be able to be running g to our own number at that time and this is a positive number to be the outcome for us all.

I have seen people sentenced under opposing parallels and this is so devisive as to call all family away from the afflicted decent and honest person. Bullying of the gang of the common man from car purchasing to oil bearing and giving numbers for purchasing requirements in this World is legally tied-properties of man's two pences; and is why innocence in man is regarded uselessly and humbly as a non-starter and humble being thus disregarded whereas men sometimes don't care so much of disregard in daily life. There is a predilection occurring of their friendship not being able to be seen. The knock-on impact being debilitating depression.

It's so hard to be depressed so that the dun can't shine on you and the warmth makes you ring within water. The assumption being the consumption less of food, drink, beer and whey. This human in us all is encouraged to It's detriment in childhood so as to glare in on us in adulthood, now where we are being controlled as too many wrongs mean no tea for us; as more prison hostels are required for when we are grown up; Innocence means we have childhood experience of life late into our adulthood.

We are propelled into being cool and then we are demonstrated to our death walking ever onwards stronger to our coolness, in the tomb of a living-graveyard. There have been many burials in life and we all know one of them; childbirth is being distorted ss a perversion currently and poor mother lying their in pain and unknowing; know the pain, no the money for you are warned and you can't gain.

We have gone preposterous and eye conditions borne in the womb along limb defects come to us next, for our difficulties rise, to stand along. Cataracts and Traucoma come from stretching preposterous and limb defects come from Mercury.

Indeed there was a move to make people unable to marry. A very kind man helped me to give my first refusal to put a foot on that and years later it may come back to haunt our general notion of God ours consensional.

Best not to leave it there though forever again we are given a choice of change either to drop the gauntlet or carry on the World Cup again. Hear the news on a daily basis and change your needs accordingly. Four we will folloew MATTHEW MARK LUKE and JOHN.

A book of manners which Is already condemned, what chance is that but name.

Shit, Shit, you care said my Mother; down the phone went, my nerves went shattered so I had to dare to leave it there by my trothe my husband said. Your life is your own now, I recollect my Mother's saying; your truthe is you will not dare. Probably true, as I won't go against a certain level.

Austria say those are true Mothers' words. When a man in a marriage circle dies, the rest of the circle has to divorce and Austria see the sense in that in what it is. My stepfather, Richard died and my mother was grievous because he had to die to her in my life with her. I was very muddled by that deceased thought when sometimes he was still alive and she loves him and so also had to divorce. This is Austria's Law of parental guidance, where the children are lost in a marriage. I was told this in Austria in a Boulangerie, where I had Ordered an alcoholic cake, that cutt my throate.

Now years later I meet a friend who is going through the same Austrian British law to divorce her husband because sadly one of her husband's has died. The depression has caused fit's and diabetes and depression of her family whom do not know if my friend is even rational or not. Of, course, she is rational but ties remain tight. This is the reason why Britain need to loosen ties with the Austrian-British Law.

Diet is the next one with cherry tomatoes one at a time with an extra one if you feel like dancing with the Devil. VitaminB12 Riboflavin is not something everyone wishes to take due to Religious reasons but the odd Cherry Tomato makes a good absorption of the product and this with little gem lettuce is all many of us need to take on our spring to daily summer diet. The change of the seasons diet is vital to adhere to, in increasing salads.

Women have only their own knowledge of their inner flush and have got to know when to push their man off when they get to close to them in their inner flush. Men who refuse to do this need a few loving words to know when to leave off because the strength of yourself is what you need in intercourse.

Men need to take these kind words within the loving of their relationship. Your reaction exists within you; so where you came from exists in your speech response and should be adhered to thee, in this sense of reaction. In this the sexual bafflement is over.

Lamentations do occur sometimes at this stage when two partners do not meet speechables. This is a natural exposition of ending their achievement to love one another. Due concordance and recompense may to occur to the couple, through life insurance and in the decree of divorce; to thee settlement. Especially when a liking to dicing with death incurrs to one or each of the partners in the settlement. This keeps a man's altercations in sensitivities.

In a world of sugar bat arguments can flare when someone's called a honeyed bat. This of an occasion where dating in your mid-fifties is a no-no, so loneliness and isolation settles on the life-changing process of a woman. One community can flare at this annunciation and cause a fight-on for many years and has probably affected many a community in this World. It is probably why Palestine invaded Israel this past year of 2023. Natural causes could have ended this dispute on a numbers a date since passed.

Are Women such a hoaring as to be devoid of emotional requirement; in this World of orderly compassion; the answer is clearly no. To have fought on for so long over a love story is to copy;copy index fatigue and this goes against the Geneva Contract.

Will the World be good enough to give enough enriched Silver in Nitrite to the atomic devastation, should Russia send the bomb over Israel. Going on the demands of Japan to remembering, perhaps Israel won't want Silver Nitrate for the sky or Silver Nitrite for the earth.

We are looking at death in the face, so carry on and keep on. Even purity condemns with a very harsh hand. We are all parsimonious as we decide on going with our innate power which of the two sides we expose in our response; either wit or compassion. Therefore we are not fit to expose ourselves to nuclear activity via atomic bombing of an area or Country. We are not fit and we live within this, but by God's power we submit to life and the choices within life. So we still need him and we do as his forms of us still do need to exist; forevermore.

The existence of man is to fight.

One of these areas is ecology and I remember the chanting 35 years ago of break it to fix it which has been proven. Buying yourself flowers is not Buying yourself sex although plants and flowers do have photosynthesis exploitation to respire. Just like animals they know they are here to live and to come back again in on ever-on-going circle of life and death.

It is to answer yes to the noun of the man's name. However Brussels is lying and we know this is true. Many people live in lies because they find it more acceptable to configuration two of their minds. So we answer no to it. Everyone is thus included. Boulevard 18, Bruges, Belgium is a Town House where papers are signed. We may need to go and sign some papers in this picturesque little waterfront square, in the majestic and pretty facetted building. Indeed they do have a Bromide concern because of the little Dab fish in the harbour; there. The Dab fish shed their scales in the waterfront every two weeks so the mung smell is a factor of living as it is in older people or clothes in a charity shop, pervasive and strong.

Hope has met its pass and the papers have been signed. The Town House which is called Maisonettes has done its work as far as Britain is concerned.

Yeasts are grown from moulds and moulds are grown in Palestine, as papyrus is grown in the banks of the river Nile.

The story of Moses in a woven basket or cask is true of the river Nile. King David killing the first born sons is in Britain octopuses talk. This has brought back a memory to my mind and struggle and fleeing from trouble to be consequently moved from my family for thinking to and expressing a deep thought level which is ordinary to children of 8 years old.

However my father was occasioned to wince and he doesn't like that. My mother loved that within him though and stayed with him forever under a double-crossed curse; she gave to him herself first. After which I was thrown out of a car and went into a new house where I asked to be adopted. Although guidance has been fearfully strong, my physical fear of being chucked out of a car and my emotional fear of finding a new house and a new family is adaptive.

Gaye men wonder at whether it is safe to put our used sanitary towels in to the poubelle. Probably I think. The scattered emotionals are enviable by most women as seeing a woman needing support as a man, they feel their own rites to protection are less adequate in their feelings of strength. This can be displayed by arcane behaviour.

Metaphysically thee of the Church are embodied by the Holy trinity whether women or men whom could display any emotions in emotive responses, from within our lives. This is adequate meaning normal but gets us power on top of our own power and leads to a higher cost for a few seconds.

Ideas are forming in us as Lead and Slate suppliers could roof the whole World from Cornwall, over the roof to our physical body. A mind to lead the question and the brain to obey it. These starlight through our mind are increased to an explosion in teenage years and cause the most wandering in our elders in dementia. Therefore I will leave it for these men and women whom know not a person to consider Islam in men too the end of it's fulfilment.

Humanitarian means famine in each of a reciprocal equation. Therefore we must use the words additional nutrients to let Israel allow the food to pass through their borders through already organised routes. It's like a phrase we know called a stitch in 9 saves time; and in this case Britain. The example is go back and recollective your notes and apply them again to see if you are still correct.

Summing up I would say we have turned to God and Allah in our manners and have used haste in financial terms where we need to have taken time but the remit in this is the cost of developing two vaccines and having them manufactured abroad. Covid 19 cost us dear and we have lost our patience with our love as in so many cases zephyrus seems to have taken the lead in this World of the half-devil.

GANGLANDERS

· · · · · · · · · · · ·

Gangland Britain where entire families are targetted to for get therefore strike twice therefore innocence.

My life has been Ganglands in Britain, France and Austria.

I am getting accustomed ostumed too looking different.

Peoples fear of me is being submitted to an internal systems of filings.

I am starting to talk at a social center at Lunch.

I call lunch Dinner when I go to the Assynt Center.

The cycle in the World is good and bad; this gives the World its polarity and is inevitable to humankind:Law creetes.

In avoiding it and diverloging it we gain our learning and understanding of Life where we are the bait and tackle.

The music stanza is the Six:-

1. SOPRANOS
2. STOCATTOS
3. ALTOS
4. TENORS
5. DRAFTE
6. DRUMM

The implosion of masse in techno vibrancy.

Be happy for it.

REPUBLICAN RITES

· · · · · · · · · · · · · ·

30th March 2024

Israel got paid out of Lehmans and Sachs for financial combobulation.

Clerical error in Texas fencing which uses programming cable.

But there is no money for Israel this time. Their cable is in Texas.

Palestine want the cable for fencing.

Israel want to cut off Hamas.

In the second World War Japan got bombed by American Atomic Weapon with German Technology.

This War currently could see Israel bombed by Russia. There has been serious condemnation.

Mossad might fight .U.S.A.

What did Israel do in the second World War?

Cable Blasts. Terrorism Involvement against pianists movement. Some fought in Italy with British Forces and some attacked British Forces. Italy gave America U.S.A. the atomic Technology: 1954 zionists; they were called. SN^{38}-.SOLENOID.26.TIN.

We are all culturally too advanced for this.x2.52.

What happened in 1952?

Doing it the servile way. Republican Movement. The Queen was head of the Senate. Eisenhower Dwight.D. Republican became President.

Republicans are happy with the general status quo at the moment and they are all about that.

Japan had 1943 Italy surrendering to the Allies with immediately hostility from Japan.

Emotional's thoughts when dealings with DIPLOMATS in War can become suddenly rigid mortars.

Italy wanted possession of North Africa, the territories they had previously to WW1. America had received them from Britain in an agreement policy document 1880-1900. Reigning Queen Victoria.

Totally lawful for Queen Elizabeth II to be the Head of the Senate in the .U.S.A. in 1952.

India paid for Italy.

America paid for India.

Dambusting.

Republicans have decided they want to keep The Monarchy as there is a by standard to fight with after their own languages rites.

MENTAL
· · · · · ·

We are scared to be seen as nice as we are so believe it is better to be acceptable rather than admitting to sickness in the family.

Hidden for years we negate people who trust and need us to be more honest.

We are nice people and sickness is now being given the green card so after the Q+ debate everyone's acceptable because we are UT mostly.

We get post battles fatigue.

We loose our domini dominance and carry on regardless taking medication or alternative theory.

Remember our truthe? Beget or Belittle.

Remember if you are sick, you are not bad.

THE CERTAIN TIME
· · · · · · · · · · · · · · · ·

The time of the beginning is where you see your destination with your partner.

We call it the certain time.

The promises made and kept for now until DDay.

For us it was watching the TV until we frought it from them out of us.

Molested and preyed backwards into our own individual moulds by the TV.

We watch night and day.

We love ourself in eachother and hope towards the end for some relief of nothing because we all realised there would be nothing left but at least we could get better on TV. We pay the yearly fees; although now monthly on top.

We have got each other one time and another and enjoy some days out of the week but not all, as is anyone's guess.

MEN
. . .

Men go anticlockwise 3 quarters twice in rapid succession on coming. This makes them feel little.

Lead on to self rejection naturally in a man to feel safe and protected and you have a negative impact leading to impotence.

Breaking the oestrogens changing through the seminal fluid and you have an implode.

This reaction can make the obvious successful one way direction to go backwards.

The adding will is to negate this success with darkness and tension subduing excitement.

Sullen and cold will enhance a self protection hatreds to double with self rejection.

Alleviation is possible through thinking is. The thinking of vice and money is no winnings for you is one good isolation for emptiness.

To be pointed at wearing darker grey colours to suit the hair and sized is why we have circumnavigations of *our actions*.

Grey is male.

Anguish is the fine.

You are the evil.

Accept me and win if you like the person you are with.

PERCEPTION
· · · · · · · · · ·

Perceiving thought is one conversation between man and women to become parents.

Today we are pushing the pinching of people without who may seek to be In a circle different from disciplines and morales.

There the fair game of easy rituals and life on the run may seek remorse in a gambient way of processing thought.

The love we like is our own within us ourselves and many we may truly love to try the patience with ourselves.

Testing the software to meet our games of loved international we are all concerned to be within we without ourselves.

In happiness we are within ourselves and play the best in joining together the outdoor and within to measured success from ourselves and with ourselves will be the memory foam of life.

The foam of sea where we are and come into reality with the breath of reality and the force of nature.

The garden of our being from the lesions of oysters to the scum of the surface and the epidermis of the anteater.

Major Tom
· · · · · · · · ·

I was to busy too be bye and good day.

The Sargent Major rang off and fiddled with himself under the desk.

When he had finished the job he smacked his hand onto the leather improve on the table and sighed with regret.

What do you think asked the psychiatry department at the psychiatry department meeting.

We have got to lie about the that too make our monthly target meet.

Sounds like horse hunting to me said the idlest of the bunch.

A few conferred and a general convening was announced. We shall go on said the wolves leader.

The Sexual Infigdidno.

Coming Home

· · · · · · · · · · · ·

Well founded in the world way is the fact of extra marketing to the fellowship of man who is in the same variant and the wisdom of people.

A lost affair has to be paid for in a chance for peaceful renegotiate of his brain.

This makes sense to be honest with paid due.

Remember to do better than the original one of yourself.

He has been the best to you.

Too yourself to be paid by the way to go togetherness office courses of a lot of people who are all Travellers.

FELLOWSHIP

· · · · · · · · · ·

Ukraine call their people cities made of bricks and cem-mence hexa-gone 1991.

It was about Ukraine's faithful few. Hitler was of Ukraine's faith and is not renounced because he was a hit man.

Jewish meat is levie-ed free.

I think people want socialism and they are not going to get it because information technology funds the world.

We are all fighting about costs.

Heritage has become to nosey.

This bill has to be paid because it says honesty.

Men do not be friends with women because it is a riar-eity. Its' a seldom seeker and solace.

It is definitely men on top of women then.

Lost in Translation.

MEDIA FAILURE

Today we are angry looking at the graye-sky-mid-winter.

We feel haunted by ourselves and hunted by ourselves.

We are feeling well, ok, better than yesterday and nicely done.

Today the television goes on to themselves and not to us but in Media.

Today we could split our own belly open to reveal the truth of the mess of blood and vessels all split open in a mess of confused masses for everyone to see our fat cell in our true exhibitionism.

Catholics do something about the smell, protestants smell and don't do anything about it. No washing yet no washing nothing.

To Catholics Stripes are spiders and Muslim. They have not finished dealing with them yet and Jewish are Bulls yetv. This is leading to a nuclear fight bomb. It will make everything neutral again.

Doing it for the love of money is still love. Israel is waiting for the last segments of money from the war payments and they will fight on until they get their hands on their own money.

Gay people are aspeljic faithe; and they treat everyone the same way in their equal faith where they fear equal. This is the same for them as their faith is everyone. If the fight was Gaye it would be exactly the same: making the earth neutral.

Captain Pugwash.

See to Blink

· · · · · · · · · ·

The rousel is a woman's secret. To catch the ball. Stopping it and pushing it back is what a woman does, when they are behind the ball.

Pheromones decide, and they come from the biorhythms. A woman is a light to heavy bar and sometimes they will reach a high which is too much for themselves, because they are heavy and it can kill them, when they are light.

Any woman can realise their orgasms when they blink their eyelids when confined safely. Not done during ser. (to be.). Sex.

Capilliaries feed the alveoli and are the same throughout the body.

Shortness of breath is a natural consequence of this. Alleviation by medicaments is the only way; Depending on what you like the best. We all have a different tolerance to our blood.

It is in the bar way of measuring that women don't wish for orgasm as it can kill a heavy lite woman so practical alleviate is necessary and satisfaction happens to cause the languishing happiness of see.

2 you and me: In it together. In case of bullying, don't let a man start again, just carry on from before as the same time stops it from reoccurrence.

Addiction to sex is to love to tension suffocation, just vesicles and the high of less oxygen causing feeling of the thighs leading to fighting. Circular distraction. Also this is the circle of domestic violence.

Hungary Budapest

2 you and me: In it together. In case of bullying in it together. The two sides of the brain.

Hungary Budapest.

We send all our fines there. The home of music is the lyre on its own and can play the sweetest music and cause the most damage for our pockets, as it is too good for us.

To lie, cheat and steal is obvious to us. Our poor food to accommodate more, height. In the charge to kill ourselves more quickly we like the rotation of the cycle of life, to be hungry, to charge around with inspired lust.

The path of Life

A decision is practical and has to be met too. Clerical error has to be adhered to and can lead to the wrong-doing further down the line criss crossing over and followed to its end point with to severe consequences.

People can look worse enmasse because of this top command. This is why a guilty person takes and makes a practical choice only.

A guilty person can be good, true and faithful, honest and dedicated.

Guilty or not guilty is a euphemism. This is describing the path of life.

This is why some sentences can look lite in accordance with the order where the people are basically innocent.

FIRES
· · · ·

A coal fell out of the fire. It was 1969 and everything was synthetic. The lady lost her house. Life was moving on every night in the Mother's lifetime. Loneliness since her Mother's death and without counsel at the age of 8 years. She looked to her sister to learn something of growing up.

The boy started the fire in the back room of the hall. The door was padlocked to prevent a backdraft. The police let him off for Life. There was an illegality.

The tramp in the haystack sleeping peaceful and quiet; the council house man called Brent set the haystack alight. It was 1978. He had an argument with the euragena of the Life of the tramp.

Delivered
· · · · · · · · ·

Why did the man cross the road?

Because he saw a man who owed him a fiver coming his way?

Well it was the icing bag said yes.

Why did the man cross the road?

Because of the man he owed a fiver coming towards him.

Well it was of a punch drink.

Why did the woman cross the road?

Because the man changes at a distance.

Well she favoured the piece.

Why did the woman cross the road?

Because she fancied a drink with the stranger approaching.

Well she was otherwise concerned.

Why did the dog cross the road?

Wow what was that smell over there.

Well the dodgy thing one does.

Why did the man cross the road?

Because the woman caught his smell.

Why did the man cross the road?

Because the woman was tripping.

Why did the man cross the road?

Because the woman gave him a handshake.

Why did the man cross the road?

To collect his dog.

After this it turns violent.

We are willing to be sent to dusts by our man. We are willing for the pain to come with our anyone brain and just like the man calculates our line and measurements consistently with what he approves of for his particular purpose so we approach him with our anyone conversation. The heater within us all fans our desire to clench our fight between our two brain's speech.

The way we line up our congresses is too our own demise death in event of sadness where we don't look beyond our lines of defence in our abject fear of losing our striations of strength where we draw the line is up to us as it is us ourselves to let another killer go out of jail to suit themselves in their own life and it can be anyone.

All Happy
· · · · · · · ·

We are chattering bones, chicken chilling ourselves into our independent living lives.

Chattels we are in keeping our distance and being told so to do.

Loneliness is not there if only you tell yourself to be yourself in the abandon of a servant's life.

The long is happiness in your own spirit. We are creating Worldwide ourselves in our true independence with courage and support to keep ourselves to ourselves and have the wealth of contempt to go with it.

We are promoting our manners to others and no more than that exists.

The reason for our happiness is the ethereals of God creating us with all he had in the same form.

Same does not go with the same polarity so keep yourself busy to do God's work in being alone too within yourselves.

Travelling Communion

Hideous is the movement of people and the movement of people in two separate genealogy.

The immigrants are not in this group and nor is the general wc movement.

Happily we see these genuine people trapping through our lands of common good wealth informed to treat their housing as camps.

Therefore finding we are a passageway too towards their next goal in life as well as their sharing of folklore in with their travels too a greater domestic.

For the visual context it is some kind of hopefully for betterment that we all pass through exchanges with each other and in due cordially reverresent along our due courcourse with them.

The passage of travelling through this experience of exchanges holds us higher than some would wish both in culture which they think should be simpler and more cost which is always avaricious too all of us.

Today the same old fights of too whom is going to paye for all of this and we are pitiful in with how too offend and accept.

We can fix this by being damaged, dumped and delirious.

EXPRESSION

· · · · · · · · · ·

It was a dry day when the grandmother died.

Short and buxom as she was, it came across that she was not daily fit and this became a lingering cold.

The jealous man of loss of character on his own life of spin and thrift came upon financial disaster and was made to walk in the wake of his disintegration.

Jealousy leads to anger and fighting yourself in a visual expression you are not aware of in any way.

Jealousy leads to economic difficulties.

The wife had sold the workhouse penny for some stamps. They looked attractive and a bold indifference came along with the bashful exchange.

Life comes back to life again in this effervescent life as we are all internal reflections of light in the prism we hold.

HOME
. . . .

Horrah, Hoorah, we got there.

Housekeeper is situated.

I'm just a voice vocal chord.

G+flat is my sweet home.

Grey and dismal against the wind of the Atlantic.

We keep it a mucky treasure hunt inside with ticks and tacks all over the place.

A joyous resonating reeling from next door appears on a Sunday night as my husband resonates against in baffles.

We feed and swallow the dear process of wildlife planning to eaten in this pastures.

Infront of us is the ever banging washing lines of other neighbours deciding what to decry our sightseeing with in each summer.

The passing of the oarsmen though yellow they may be does not constitute a national insurance policy of which we might face at the end of this war in this ages of people transportation.

Our years of 16 have become 15 years of marriage and I may say pleasingly so with our engaging of fighting for the whole family of the world of flowers and containers.

CAROLINE MACLEOD

The brick a bracket of garages facing our Seaview and protecting us from the West wind of the North plummeting Sheila's of ice and snowing from Greenland.

Our recumbent house guest of our house is called Black Shelia and gathers me to her protection of love and direction to come gather here and sleeping and sleep.

Love of the candyfloss whatever it may mean too you is to me like the melodrama of life.

The Plateaued earth of the summer of Spain is responsible for our weathered features. We all love this in whichever way we meet with them and excited thought in any day.

Moving to the repopulate of the earth the insurances needed for the passage across the Channel Islands is gathered in the data of the Dam of great thoro'we.

The movement of lands lover's on to the sea-like explore of retirement regalia in the delight of some new irrigation on the mind of the most famous mass movements for years of tenuous re-behaviouring.

The warmth of the body outlying to the skin makes for a forever exposing habit of the wing of the wind. The cold acceptance of the body controls the euphoria of change to the body as the reminding falls of blood and regulations sweet us too a more temperate measure.

It will be for your betterment we are told and remus by in your body and you are will to your lost and found.

At this point we are leading to our own regards of square or rectangle or hexagon.

Windows against the prevailing wind of colour and shield faces us with their questions of were here before rondo lightning of us all being also with one other.

The green colour so overlays the transient mind of acceptance betterment for us too accept grey like the sky.

The colossus of our brain matter is cream with a nothing in the integral birth chamber where we are prodded and poked too natural delivery of goodness kind and gentle and life on living.

DIFFERENCE
· · · · · · · · · ·

Bleacgh pain is for the growing number of people who like the pretty color of blood.

This is a happy one thought in people who self-harm.

Colour as an artist enjoyments of is known to be inspirational.

I am an artist with Colour.

We like to self-ex our relationships first and then Relig.

I don't know the young expressionists today 2023 however I can guess that self-identity is like of oneself.

Painting by numbers was my beginning with the mechanism of jigsaws.

The freedom is immediate and talent is taught.

When we tightly hold each other innocent is an expression of joy and nudity.

We go on living and call it death but really it is a continuance of the circles of life.

Withholding is the sweetests fine landings associated with the pretties of colour.

Lucy Letby

· · · · · · · · ·

There was a doctor at the two top tier stage and that means it is filled by two doctors.

A lassie fancied one of the top who filled her promise with a half and a two job which she more than easily realised too.

The other top two doctor was behind the patents of said died baby because it was on its way out but sweetly it should be let to go.

The girl did as she was asked.

Midwifery thank you because there are so many babies too poorly to go on.

The parents were so upset for the first tooto weeks after the baby's birth that 1 baby became noted as 14 registered. 7 deaths and 7 attempted deaths.

The doctor behind the fancy answered to the 2nd top midwifery houseman, a woman nurse registered to the hospital.

There were containers at the top but really it was all to do with hospital drugs being mixed with street allowances where they are heavy bars. Arranging delivery from direct supply of The Gold Coast, Australia.

Milton Keynes UK
Ingram Content Group UK Ltd.
UKHW041455121024
449426UK00001B/112

9 798895 183120